JUST GRANDMA, GRANDPA, AND ME

BY MERCER MAYER

RANDOM HOUSE 🏠 NEW YORK

Little Critter, Mercer Mayer's Little Critter, and Mercer Mayer's Little Critter and Logo are registered trademarks of Orchard House Licensing Company. All rights reserved.

Published in the United States by Random House Children's Books, a division of Penguin Random House LLC, New York, and in Canada by Random House of Canada, a division of Penguin Random House Ltd., Toronto. The stories in this collection were originally published separately in the United States by Golden Books, an imprint of Random House Children's Books, New York, in 1983 and 1985. Random House and the colophon are registered trademarks of Penguin Random House LLC. The material contained in this book was taken from the following Golden Books publications: *Just Grandma and Me* book, characters, text, and images © 1983 by Mercer Mayer, and *Just Grandpa and Me* book, characters, text, and images © 1985 by Mercer Mayer.

Visit us on the Web!
randomhousekids.com
littlecritter.com

Library of Congress Cataloging-in-Publication Data is available upon request.

ISBN 978-0-553-53986-8

Printed in the United States of America

10 9 8 7 6 5 4 3

JUST GRANDMA AND ME
BY MERCER MAYER

We went to the beach,
just Grandma and me.

I wanted to set up the beach umbrella,

but the wind was too strong.

I flew my kite instead.

I bought hot dogs for Grandma and me,
but they fell in the sand.
So I washed them off.

I found a nice seashell for Grandma,
but it was full of a crab.

I wanted to blow up my sea horse,
but I didn't have enough air.
So Grandma helped a little.

I told Grandma to take me
way out in the deep water,

but not too far.

I put on my fins and my mask
and showed Grandma how I can snorkel.

I dug a hole in the sand for Grandma.
Then I covered her up and tickled her toes.

I built a sandcastle just for Grandma,
but a big wave came.

Grandma said that's what happens
to sandcastles, and we will build
a new one next time.

On the way home Grandma was tired,
so I told her I would watch for our stop.

We had a good time at the beach,
just Grandma and me.

JUST GRANDPA AND ME

My Mom said I need a new suit.

So we went to the city to buy one,
just Grandpa and me.

I bought the train tickets, but I let Grandpa pay.

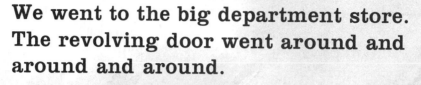

We went to the big department store.
The revolving door went around and
around and around.

We went around, too,
just Grandpa and me.

I held Grandpa's hand
so he wouldn't get lost.

He did anyway.

Lucky for Grandpa I found him right away.

CRITTER
SUITS →

We took the escalator to the
suit department.
I told Grandpa to hold on tight
to the rail.

Then Grandpa helped me choose
a shirt and tie.

Then we went to the movies.
I sat close to Grandpa
in the scary parts
so he wouldn't be afraid.

We had supper in a Chinese restaurant.
I showed Grandpa how to use chopsticks.

Then we got back on the train.
Grandpa took a nap, but not me.
I couldn't wait for Mom
to see my new suit.

We were so proud—
just Grandpa and me.